P9-CSH-302

MAC & MARIE & the TRAIN TOSS SURPRISE

by ELIZABETH FITZGERALD HOWARD

illustrations by GAIL GORDON CARTER

Four Winds Press ✲ *New York*

Maxwell Macmillan Canada *Toronto* Maxwell Macmillan International *New York* *Oxford* *Singapore* *Sydney*

Four Winds Press
Macmillan Publishing Company
866 Third Avenue
New York, NY 10022

Maxwell Macmillan Canada, Inc.
1200 Eglinton Avenue East
Suite 200
Don Mills, Ontario M3C 3N1

Macmillan Publishing Company is part of
the Maxwell Communication Group of Companies.

First edition
Printed in U.S.A.
10 9 8 7 6 5 4 3 2 1
The text of this book is set in Perpetua.
Book design by Christy Hale

Library of Congress Cataloging-in-Publication Data
Howard, Elizabeth Fitzgerald.
Mac and Marie and the train toss surprise / by Elizabeth
Fitzgerald Howard ; illustrations by Gail Gordon Carter. — 1st ed.
p. cm.
Summary: One summer evening a brother and sister eagerly
await the train that runs by their house,
wondering about the surprise their uncle
has promised them.
ISBN 0-02-744640-9
[1. Railroads—Trains—Fiction. 2. Brothers and sisters—Fiction.
3. Afro-Americans—Fiction.] I. Carter, Gail Gordon, ill.
II. Title.
PZ7.H83273Mac 1993
[E]—dc20 92-17918

ABOUT THE STORY

My father, John MacFarland (Mac) Fitzgerald, grew up in the ''Big House,'' which faced the train tracks near Patapsco, Maryland. ''Prettiest house on the line between Baltimore and Washington,'' said a letter from the Pennsylvania Railroad Company to my grandparents. Mac loved trains and dreamed about being an engineer—an impossible dream for a little African-American boy at the turn of the century, but a dream nonetheless.

This story is based on one of the many tales of childhood adventure my father shared with me.

For Paw from Beetle

—E.F.H.

ABOUT THE ILLUSTRATIONS

The illustrations in this book were done with watercolors and colored pencil on watercolor paper. The finished paintings were color-separated and printed using four-color process.

To my husband, Gary

—G.G.C.

It was beginning to get dark. Mac was sure that Marie was tired of waiting. He had watched her catch six fireflies and put them in a jelly jar, clamping the lid on tight each time. Mac had punched holes in the lid. Marie had put some grass in, too; she said it was in case the fireflies were hungry. Mac knew that Marie knew that fireflies didn't really eat grass. Marie was just playing around, trying to pass the time.

Tiger, Mac's old collie, was watching Marie, too. Tiger didn't run after fireflies. He might chase a rabbit if he smelled one. Or he might just lie there, with his ears back, lazy and comfortable. Waiting.

"It'll be soon now, Marie." Mac checked Papa's big pocket watch. "About five more minutes, if it's on time." Mac sat up straight. He had been sprawled out in the tall grass near the railroad embankment, chewing on a cat-o'-nine-tails stem. Mac wasn't as fidgety as Marie. He was older, and besides, he knew most of the train schedules by heart. Mac knew about trains.

Marie stopped chasing fireflies. She stared down the long tracks. Then she turned impatiently, twisted the lid off the fireflies jar, and dumped them out. She watched them fly away, flickering their lights.

"Hey, Mac! What if it's all a big trick?"

"But you saw Uncle Clem's letter," Mac answered.

"Maybe he's fooling us—making us all excited about some silly old surprise."

"Oh, come on, Marie. Why would he tell us exactly the name of the train and the time and everything?" What does Marie know anyway? Mac thought.

Mac pulled the scrunched-up piece of paper from his back pocket. Uncle Clem's letter. Almost too dark to read, but Mac could remember every word.

Dear Mac,

I have a summer job in the dining car on the Seaboard Florida Limited. We'll be passing by the Big House, heading back to New York, a bit after half-past eight on Thursday night. I'm going to throw something off for you. It's for Marie, too. Wrapped in white paper and tied with string. Just be sure you pick it up!

Love,

Uncle Clem

Uncle Clem was Mac's favorite relative. Uncle Clem went to college in New York. And now, even better, he had a summer job on a train.

More than anything, Mac loved trains. He wanted to ride on them, to see where those long, silvery tracks went. And when he grew up, he would get a job on the trains, too.

Marie was right, though. Sometimes Uncle Clem did play jokes, like the time no one was expecting him, and he hid in the hall closet all through dinner and then jumped out during dessert and almost scared Mama and Marie out of their wits! Mac had thought that was a pretty funny trick.

But this wouldn't be a trick. Not tonight.

"What's it going to be, Uncle Clem's surprise?" Marie asked. "If he's working in the dining car, what's it going to be?"

"Maybe some steak they don't need," Mac said. But he didn't really think so.

"Hey, Mac, what about a big chocolate cake? Or maybe a pie?"

"Better be squash pie," Mac teased. "It'll sure squash when it lands in the bushes."

Marie laughed.

Mac stared down the tracks as far as he could. He had lived close to the train tracks almost since he could remember, and now he was nine. Papa had bought the Big House—everyone called it that—when Mac was still practically a baby. It was a nice house. Once Mama got a letter from the railroad people saying the Big House was the prettiest place on the line between Baltimore and Washington.

Mac liked the house, especially the two big porches. The one in front was called the Flower Porch. You could sit there and admire Mama's flower garden. Now the garden was full of daylilies and hollyhocks. The second porch, the best porch, on the back, Mac had named the Train Porch. It faced the railroad tracks. There you could wait for the trains to come. Watch them zoom by. Mac liked it at night, too. Lying upstairs in bed he'd listen for the far-off whistle and then the *clack-a-clacky* sounds of the night trains speeding past.

There were a few local trains just between Baltimore and Washington. They were shorter and slower and stopped at little towns like Laurel and Halethorpe and Patapsco, near the Big House. But the long trains, the really fast trains, went north to Boston, even to Bar Harbor, Maine. And on the other track, they went south, through Washington, D.C., and Virginia, and both Carolinas, and Georgia, ending up in Florida. Mac knew the names of all the long trains. The Merchants Limited. The Royal Blue Flyer. The Federal. The Colonial. The Florida Fast Mail. The Keystone Express. The New York Special. And Uncle Clem's train, the Seaboard Florida Limited.

Someday, someday . . . Mac would be working on those trains. Going everywhere. Seeing the world. Way up north to Bar Harbor, Maine. Way down south. To Florida. Maybe out west, even. California! And not working in the dining car, like Uncle Clem, even though Uncle Clem was the luckiest person in the world. I'm going to be a fireman, and then I'm going to be an engineer, Mac thought.

"Hey, Mac! Mac! What time is it?" Marie asked.

Mac squinted at Papa's watch. "Twenty-five minutes to nine." Three more minutes now. But would Uncle Clem really throw something off? Mac worried a little bit. If it was food, would that be right? Would it be leftovers? Maybe from people's plates? No, Uncle Clem wouldn't do that. Unless it was a bone for Tiger. But Uncle Clem had said it was something for him and Marie.

"It's so quiet," Marie said. "I can hear a worm walking. I can hear ants dancing. I can hear moles moving in their holes."

"Just nighttime noises," Mac said softly.

A whippoorwill called out.

An owl hooted.

Swoosh!

"What was that? A bat?" Marie moved closer to Mac.

"Listen! Listen!" Mac said suddenly. "Can you hear it now?"

A train whistle whined way down the tracks.

"All right! That's it!" Mac shouted.

"That's it!" Marie echoed. "Be careful, Mac!"

The round light on the front of the engine grew larger and larger and brighter and brighter. The whistle grew louder. There was smoke and whirling sparks and the hissing of steam.

"Yippee!" Mac yelled. He counted the cars flashing by. "Dining car!" he shouted into the darkness. Was that a silhouette, a shadow of someone standing at the end of the dining car?

"Uncle Clem!" Mac screamed, waving his arms. And yes, there was something tossed off, something flying into the sky... something flying up and down again. "Uncle Clem! Uncle Clem!" Mac called, and the train was gone.

"I saw it!" shouted Marie. "I saw a package in the air!"

"Over this way," Mac said, scrambling down the embankment, snatching hold of slippery weeds. "You wait there, Marie. I can get it." Mac had to be careful near the tracks. At least he knew that the next train wouldn't be due for a whole hour.

Where was that package? Tiger was barking and sniffing. *Where was it?*

"Marie, I see it! I see the package!" And there, partly hidden in the weeds, was the lumpy, white bundle. Smaller than a bed pillow. Bigger than a loaf pan. Tied with brown string. Mac picked it up. He and Tiger clambered back up to Marie.

"Is it a big chocolate cake, Mac? Let me smell it!" Marie tried to pull the package out of Mac's hands.

"Doesn't feel like food, Marie. Let's take it back to the Big House to open it."

Mama and Papa were sitting in the dark on the Train Porch, drinking lemonade, waiting.

"Well, well, so Clem tossed something off for you. . . .Well, let's see it," said Papa. Mama went into the house for the oil lamp.

Mac dug and pulled at the string until he got all the knots out. Marie helped him unwrap the layers and layers of white paper. "Clem sure didn't want whatever it is to break. I've never seen so much wrapping," said Mama.

At last.

It was mottled, pinkish and brown, bumpy-rough on the outside, and smooth, shiny pink on the inside. Wider at the open end. And it curved around.

"It's a seashell!" Marie and Mac shouted in one shout. "A *giant* seashell!" Mac added. "And here's a letter, too." Tucked in the shell was a piece of folded paper. Mac read:

Dear Mac and Marie,

This is a conch shell from Florida.
Maybe you can hear the ocean.

Bye,

Uncle Clem

P.S. Watch for the train next Thursday night!

Mac smoothed his hands all over the big shell, tracing the bumps and curves with his fingers. Marie held it, too, turning it around, carefully, carefully. "Pink," she said. "Inside it's pink." Then Mac held the shell up to his ear. "I can hear it! The ocean!" he said. Marie listened, too. And so did Mama and Papa.

"Uncle Clem got you a little piece of Florida," Papa said. "Now that's a real nice surprise."

Mac listened some more to the ocean sound. He smiled at the beautiful shell. He smiled at Mama and Papa and Marie. "When I'm an engineer on the train to Florida," he said, "I'm going to bring back surprises from the world, too—just like Uncle Clem."